ACCOLADES FOR THE
ALDO ZELNICK COMIC NOVEL SERIES

An alphabetical adventure for middle-grade readers 7 to 13

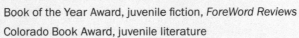

Book of the Year Award, juvenile fiction, *ForeWord Reviews*

Colorado Book Award, juvenile literature

Mountains & Plains Independent Booksellers Association Regional Book Award

Creative Child magazine Seal of Excellence

Indiebound Kids' Indie Next List selection

Independent Publisher Silver "IPPY" Award

Creative Child magazine Preferred Choice Award

Quid Novi Award, first prize

Moonbeam Children's Book Award, silver medal for comic/graphic novel

Top 10 Educational Children's Products - Dr. Toy

Book of the Year Award, kids' fiction, *Creative Child* magazine

Moonbeam Children's Book Award, silver medal for activity book

"Every library that serves Wimpy Kid fans (which, honestly, is every library, period) should have the Aldo Zelnick series on its shelves."
— Katie Ahearn, children's librarian, Washington DC

"Aldo is an endearing narrator. His deadpan sense of humor is enjoyable even for adults. Each book is a fast-paced, light read, perfect for the kid looking for a transition from comics to chapter books."
— Sarah, children's buyer, Left Bank Books

"When I am reading an Aldo Zelnick book in RTI, I don't want to go back to my classroom. Somehow I want to keep reading...and I don't like reading."
— an elementary student

"I am completely charmed by this series. The drawings and text have the quality of simultaneously being appealing to children and also amusing for adults. A big strength here is in the development of the characters. This is wonderful, since this is going to be an A to Z series and we'll have plenty of time to get to know them better. These are individuals with staying power. With the sketchbook comes a wonderful, not-overstated message of allowing Aldo to be himself and follow his creativity. Bravo!"
— Jean Hanson

"...a must for your elementary school reader."
— Christy, Reader's Cove bookstore

"In the wake of Wimpy Kid and Amelia's Notebooks comes Aldo Zelnick. Oceanak has created a funny and lively hero. The illustrations add to the humor."
— *Library Media Connection*

Kerfuffle

AN ALDO ZELNICK COMIC NOVEL

Written by Karla Oceanak

Illustrated by Kendra Spanjer

BAILIWICK PRESS

Also by Karla Oceanak and
Kendra Spanjer — Artsy-Fartsy,
Bogus, Cahoots, Dumbstruck,
Egghead, Finicky, Glitch,
Hotdogger, Ignoramus, Jackpot,
All Me, All the Time

Copyright © 2015 by Karla Oceanak and Kendra Spanjer

Published by:
Bailiwick Press
309 East Mulberry Street
Fort Collins, Colorado 80524
(970) 672-4878
Fax: (970) 672-4731
www.bailiwickpress.com
www.aldozelnick.com

Manufactured by:
Bang Printing, Brainerd, Minnesota, USA
July 2015

Book design by:
Launie Parry
Red Letter Creative
www.red-letter-creative.com

ISBN 978-1-934649-53-4

Library of Congress Control Number: 2015908957

24 23 22 21 20 19 18 17 16 15   7 6 5 4 3 2 1

Dear Aldo—
Since your J sketchbook
is kaput,* my little
kumquat,* it's
time to kickstart* K!
Kisses, Goosy

ALDO,

"An investment in knowledge
pays the best interest,"
Benjamin Franklin once said.

So keep learning! Also, shall
we try karaoke* this month?

– Mr. Mot

WHO'S WHO

ME—
SIR ALDO ZELNICK.
KINGLY KNIGHT.

TIMOTHY, MY
KNUCKLEHEAD* OF
A BIG BROTHER.

MY CHIVALROUS BEST FRIENDS,
SIR JACK LOPEZ AND DAME BEE GOODE.

MY PARENTS, A.K.A. MOM AND DAD.

KARL, TIMOTHY'S
NEW FRIEND AND
POSSIBLE KNAVE.*

MR. MOT, FENCER, NEIGHBOR, WORD NERD, AND FRIEND.

GOOSY, MY CREATIVE GRANDMA.

BACON BOY, MY OWN COMIC SUPERHERO, AND HIS TRUSTY SQUIRE, C.W.

WITH SPECIAL GUEST APPEARANCES BY:

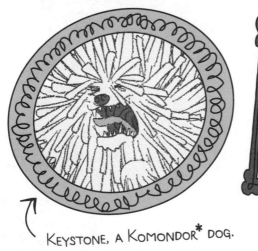

KEYSTONE, A KOMONDOR* DOG.

THE EASTER BUNNY'S KEISTER.*

Ye Olde A-Z Book Kiosk*

COME HITHER!

WELCOMETH TO BOOKETH K IN MINE ALPHABETICAL SERIES! DON'T FORGETTETH TO WATCHETH FOR *.
THEN GO THITHER TO THE WORD GALLERY AT THE BACKETH OF THE BOOK TO SEE WHAT THE WORD MEANETH.

AS THE STORY PROCEEDETH, THOU MUST REMEMBER THAT I, MAXIMILIAN ZELNICK, AM THE ORIGINAL AND MOST RIGHTFUL PET IN THIS BEAUTEOUS SERIES.

APRIL FOOL

This morning when my alarm went off, I tried to hit the snooze button, as usual, but I couldn't move my hands! I yanked my arms out from under my pillow, where they were sleeping, and saw that my wrists were looped together with a handkerchief. What?!

I pulled off the handkerchief with my teeth, hushed the alarm, and zombie-shuffled to the bathroom. I frowned at myself in the mirror, as usual, because of it being a school morning. Stuck to my left cheek, where nothing but skin (and possibly cookie crumbs) had been the night before was a humongous rub-on tattoo of a jaunty kangaroo.* Oh, c'mon!

Then I hustled to the business end of the
bathroom, as usual. As I lifted the plastic sitting
ring and, uh, launched Number 1, droplets went
spraying all over the place like a lemonade fountain
because SOMEONE HAD STRETCHED PLASTIC
WRAP OVER THE TOILET OPENING!

THE OLD PLASTIC
WRAP TRICK:
AMUSING OR
ABOMINABLE?
IT DEPENDS ON
WHERE YOU
STAND ON APRIL
FOOLS' DAY.

"Ahhhhhhhh!" I yelled in my emergency voice. "What! Is! Going! On!!!"

That's when my teenager brother, Timothy, made his appearance.

APRIL FOOLS, BRO! BETTER GET SCRUBBIN'—YOUR FACE <u>AND</u> THE FLOOR, LOOKS LIKE—OR YOU'LL BE LATE FOR SCHOOL.

"Mommm!" was my next logical yell.

One kinda good/kinda bad thing about moms is that even on April 1st, they'll only put up with so much nonsense. Today it was good, because Mom made Timothy wipe up and disinfect the bathroom while I de-kangarooed my face.

But *grrr*. Timothy! I am <u>so</u> getting back at him after school.

Today was Friday, so school had that loose, start-of-the-weekend feeling, like when a dress-up activity is over and, <u>finally</u>, I get to unbuckle the belt Mom made me wear. Plus, Mr. Krug (he's my teacher) announced that the Medieval Faire is coming. And he wasn't even April Foolsing us!

HEAR YE! HEAR YE! BE IT KNOWN THAT THE DANA ELEMENTARY MEDIEVAL FAIRE FOR ALL KNIGHTS, KNAVES,* AND MAIDENS OF GRADE THE 5TH SHALL COME TO PASS ON FRIDAY THE 29TH DAY OF APRIL. YOUR ATTENDANCE IS MOST RESPECTFULLY REQUESTED. PLEASE DRESS IN PERIOD ATTIRE FOR A DAY OF REVELRY, MERRIMENT, AND FEASTING! P.S. AS ALWAYS, BEWARE OF DRAGONS.

Then, to get us in the medieval mood, he started reading a book out loud to us called *The Sword in the Stone*, which is about knights and quests and castles, etc.

So after the closing bell rang, my best friend, Jack, and I hoisted our backpacks and headed straight for our fort, which is in our neighborhood under a giant pine tree. That's where we go to do all our Important Thinking.

"The Medieval Faire... I've been looking forward to it my entire life," mused Jack, sitting down and stretching out his toothpicky legs. "Every spring since kindergarten,* all we could do was stand there and watch the 5th graders have an awesome party that we weren't invited to. But now, finally, we're the 5th graders!"

"Yes," I agreed. "Now it's our turn to be special. Actually, I've been special all along..."

"You know what, though?" continued Jack. "Now that <u>we</u> get to be the knights, I'm getting this knightly feeling." His words suddenly sounded grand and generous. "Like we need to <u>do</u> special things between now and the party. I mean, knights are all about quests and fighting for what's right—not having parties for no reason."

"That's dumb," I pointed out. "Having parties for no reason is the <u>best</u> reason to have parties." I might not have been making sense, but at least I was standing up for what I believed in. "And...isn't practically being done with elementary school a great reason?"

"Exactly! That's what I mean!" said Jack. "We're the big kahunas* now, so, like, we should be good examples to the little kids. You know—we're large and in charge..."

"You are <u>not</u> large," I scoffed. "You're so skinny you could hula hoop with a Fruit Loop. Plus, you <u>hate</u> fighting! You avoid conflict like I avoid cardio."

Just then we heard a crunchy, branchy noise. It was Bee, our-friend-who-happens-to-be-a-girl, coming to join us. Jack and I are the fort founders, but Bee is a bona fide member too. And sometimes, like today, she brings leftover pizza from her parents' restaurant.

"Are you guys as fired up about the Medieval Faire as I am?" asked Bee as she set the pizza box on the pine-needly ground and slid it to me. "I hear we get to play Capture the Flag and do a special dance!"

"Sounds ambitious," I said, munching on a delectable slice of pepperoni with little blobs of green stuff. "I hear we get to feast and drink from golden goblets covered in jewels. And then there's Jack, who thinks that if we're going to be knights, we should <u>do good</u> deeds. Pffft."

"Oooh, that's a noble idea," said Bee. "Like a quest! What should we do?" She tore off a piece of pizza and nibbled. "Isn't this kale* delicious?"

Kale. So that's what the green blobs were. "The answers to your questions," I said, swallowing, "are 'Nothing' and 'Weirdly, yes.'"

Pretty soon our thirstiness drove us from the fort in a quest for water. As we crawled out from the fort, we saw Timothy and his new friend, Karl, on the playground. They were going down the slide standing up...in their socks.

I THOUGHT I HAD GOOD BALANCE, BUT YOU'RE CLEARLY THE MASTER.

YEAH. I LEARNED HOW TO WALK WHEN I WAS 3 DAYS OLD.

APRIL FOOLS!

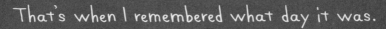

That's when I remembered what day it was.

LET'S STEAL THEIR SHOES.

WHY?

BECAUSE IT'S APRIL FOOLS! AND TIMOTHY PRANKED ME BIG-TIME THIS MORNING.

SO, WE'LL BE MAKING A WRONG THING RIGHT?

EXACTLY! THINK OF IT AS... AS A KNIGHTLY CRUSADE.

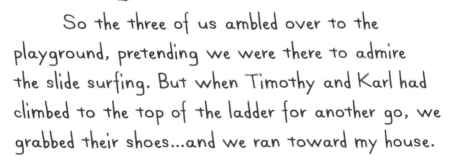

So the three of us ambled over to the playground, pretending we were there to admire the slide surfing. But when Timothy and Karl had climbed to the top of the ladder for another go, we grabbed their shoes...and we ran toward my house.

I had one of Timothy's sneakers. Since I'm missing the speed gene, Timothy and Karl caught up to me first. Timothy tore the shoe from my hands and kept running, but I sure admired the muddiness of his socks and the irk of his smile as he sped past me.

In my driveway Timothy closed in on Jack. How did Jack respond to this test of his courage? Right away he hot-potatoed Timothy that other sneaker like it was gonna melt his fingers off. Some bravery.

That left Bee with both of Karl's shiny black shoes. "April Fools!" she giggled, and she kept on running.

"You think you're funny?" Karl said, looking more apoplectic by the minute as he chased Bee, who was buzzing around the yard like the insect she's named after.

"Catch me if you can!" she sang. Then she stopped a safe ways away from Karl and said, "Hey! Where'd you get these kicks*? They're Kapers!"

"Hand 'em over!" snarled Karl. Now his voice sounded rough, like Jack's rock tumbler when it's tumbling, and even though he's twice Bee's size, he <u>lunged</u> for her...

20

That's when my dad stepped out onto the front porch. He must have heard the commotion. "Anyone hungry for some just-baked Snickerdoodles?" he called.

Karl, inches away from K.O.-ing* Bee, instantly dropped his arms to his sides and flipped his face from mean to nice. Bee held out the sneakers to Karl, who took them then followed Timothy and Dad inside.

"Did you see that?" said Jack when it was just us and Bee in the driveway. "That guy was about to go ballistic over a little April Fools' joke! If your dad hadn't shown up just then..."

I shrugged. "All I know is his name's Karl and he's on the high school baseball team with Timothy," I said. "I've seen him maybe twice."

"His family must be super rich," said Bee. "I saw those sneakers in *Sports Illustrated for Kids*. They cost 400 dollars! And also, I wasn't afraid of him. At least, not very."

I whistled low and long. "400 bucks for shoes to run in?! That's kooky.* Shoes you <u>can't</u> run in might be worth 4 bills on fitness testing days..."

Jack straightened his spine and rolled his shoulders back. He lifted his chin slightly. "If Karl is a knave, we must be on guard," he said as serious as toast without butter. "As knights, we are bound to not only do good deeds but protect our friends and neighbors from bad ones. This is our sacred oath."

Solemnly, Jack held out his right hand, palm down. Bee placed her hand kitty-corner* across his. I looked from Jack to Bee and back again. Their expressions were very *Fellowship of the Ring*. I decided that adding my hand to the stack would be the fastest way to get to the warm Snickerdoodles waiting inside.

ALL FOR ONE AND ONE FOR ALL! (UNLESS WE'RE TALKING ABOUT COOKIES... THEN THEY'RE ALL FOR ME!)

CHAPTER II

Knights in BROWN Cardboard

Where do you go when you need a knightly suit of armor on a kid budget? Well I don't know where <u>you</u> go, but <u>I</u> go to Goosy's.

In case you didn't realize, Goosy is my grandma. She's an artsy-fartsy type with a knack* for costumes. Second-grade Halloween she made me into a ketchup* bottle so legit I had a French-fry addiction for weeks.

Anyways, Jack and Bee and I walked to Goosy's house this morning as regular kids but marched home as knights in kinda shiny, kinda colorful armor.

The secret? Cardboard. Lots and lots of cardboard. And duct tape. Oh, and paint.

GOOSY MAKES ALL <u>KINDS</u> OF COOL STUFF IN HER ART STUDIO.

While Goosy cut the cardboard and we painted, we blabbed about the Medieval Faire and how us 5th graders would get to eat turkey legs and probably joust and do falconry and fire catapults and stuff like that.

"I <u>love</u> turkey legs!" I said. "I've noticed that they're the only large meat that's socially acceptable to eat with your hands. Plus, you're allowed to walk around while you chew on one..."

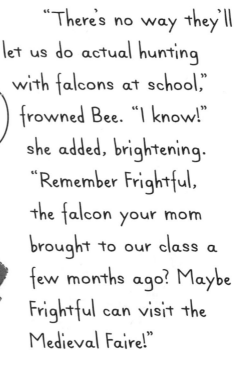

KNOCK KNOCK.

WHO IS IT, MY LITTLE KNISH*?

NEIL.

NEIL WHO, DEAR?

KNEEL* BEFORE THE KING!

"There's no way they'll let us do actual hunting with falcons at school," frowned Bee. "I know!" she added, brightening. "Remember Frightful, the falcon your mom brought to our class a few months ago? Maybe Frightful can visit the Medieval Faire!"

"I think I can win at jousting," said Jack. "Skinny targets are hard to hit."

"I'm thrilled to see you kids so keyed up* about history and school!" said Goosy. "This is what happens when you add art and theater to book learning. It comes alive!"

"Wait, who are the bad guys going to be?" asked Jack. "I mean, knights joust with other knights as a sport, but they also fight real battles against bad guys, right?"

The words "bad guys" made me remember Karl's freak-out yesterday. For those few seconds, he'd seemed more evil than a fire-breathing dragon. It gave me the heebie-jeebies. To change my brain subject, I noticed Bee. "Hey, you're being a <u>knight</u>?" I asked her. "Whatever happened to damsels in distress?"

FOR YOUR INFORMATION, I'M NOT <u>IN</u> DISTRESS. I <u>CAUSE</u> DISTRESS.

While we waited for the paint on the cardboard to dry, we snacked on kiwi* fruit Goosy cut up and we played Kerplunk.* Guess which distressing knight won? Then we strapped on our new suits of armor and headed for Castle Zelnick.

WHO MADE <u>YOU</u> KING?

NOW COME THE DAYS OF KING VALENTINE. MAY THEY BE BLESSED.

OH PLEASE. KINGS AREN'T MADE; WE'RE BORN.

P.S. WHAT THEY DON'T TELL YOU ABOUT BEING KING IS: WITH GREAT PRIVILEGE COMES GREAT RESPONSIBILITY...

P.P.S. VALENTINE IS MY MIDDLE NAME, REMEMBER? MY FRIENDS WON'T LET ME FORGET.

CHAPTER III

seeing

IS

BELIEVING

Mom wouldn't let me wear my knight-king costume to church this morning, but as soon as we got home, I put it on. Wearing a crown is good for your self-esteem.

I'M A COWARDLY KOWTOWER.* I'LL JUST GO SIT IN THE CORNER...

BRING ME MY BACON AND MY THRONE!

As I was marching through the family room in a kingly way, Mom handed me a string of purple-green-pink-yellow plastic egg lights. "Help me decorate for Easter, my liege,*" she said.

"It's almost Easter?" I slathered the lights around the fireplace mantel, plugged them in, then stepped back to admire my artsy-fartsy skills. "I <u>love</u> Easter!" I rejoiced.

"I know you do," smiled Mom. "Yes, it's in a couple of weeks. Should we have a spiral ham for Easter dinner? Or maybe lamb chops..."

"Both!" I decreed. I landscaped the top of the mantel with clumps of pink plastic Easter grass. "And don't forget the scalloped potatoes."

"Let's swordfight, Aldo!" cried Timothy, who'd grabbed a wooden carrot from a kitschy* knick-knack* Mom had just set on the eating table. He poked me with the carrot and jumped back, poked me with it again and jumped back.

YOU NEED CARDBOARD ARMOR WITH A BROTHER LIKE MINE. SHEESH.

KA-POW!

"Cease your knavery*!" I proclaimed to Timothy. "Hark! I just heard the doorbell! It's the dictionary makers! They've come to take took your picture for the word 'knave'!"

"Say, Timothy, do you think Karl and his dad would like to join us on Easter Sunday?" asked Mom.

"Nay! Methinks Karl is evil," I tried to say king-ishly, but Timothy was being so boisterous he drowned me out. I don't think he heard Mom's question, either. He'd moved on to kickboxing* the giant stuffed bunnyrabbit Mom always puts by the fireplace at Eastertime.

Mom sighed and turned back to me. "So," she asked me gently, "do you think the Easter Bunny will come this year?"

I could feel my cheeks go as pink as the plastic grass. I didn't want to have this conversation, especially not in front of my sock-surfing, kickboxing, superjock 15-year-old brother. "The Easter Bunny is for babies," I muttered.

"He is? Are you sure?" asked Mom.

Was I sure?

"Peasants!" I yelled, changing the subject. "Can't a king get any bacon around here?"

"Good timing!" Dad called from the stove. "Sunday brunch is <u>served</u>."

As we ate and Timothy jabbered about the baseball pitch he learned this week—the knuckleball*—I let my memories float back to the time that I actually saw, with my own 2 eyeballs, the Easter Bunny...

I was little—maybe 3 or 6. I was in my bed asleep when something woke me up. It must have been super early in the morning, because the light coming in through my window was weak and gray. I remember lying there, my head still on the pillow, sleepily looking around the room and not noticing anything out of the usual. But then a hop of movement by the door caught my eye.

I sat up just in time to glimpse a white rear end and puffy tail disappearing from my view.

It's Easter, I remembered! I jumped from my bed, ran to my door, and gaped down the hallway. Nothing. I turned back to my bedroom. There, on my bookcase, lay a blue plastic egg. I ran to it and shook it. Something rattled. I pulled it apart. A fun-size Kit Kat tumbled out!

While I chewed, I looked around my room and saw more plastic eggs hiding in plain sight. Then I dashed to my parents' bedroom to wake them up and tell them the astonishing news.

After that, the story became a Zelnick family legend: The Time Aldo Saw The Easter Bunny. Whenever my parents bring it up, they're kinda teasing me, I know—like 2 parts aww-isn't-that-adorable and 1 part this-kid-is-bonkers. And Timothy...welp, if you can imagine how he harasses me about it, you can imagine how I deny, deny, deny.

But here's the thing that I can only admit in the privacy of my own sketchbook: I <u>did</u> see the Easter Bunny. I know I did! Santa and the Tooth Fairy...they're useful sometimes, but I've never had my eyeballs on them. The E.B., on the other hand, let me see his keister.*

Ever since that day, I've been hoping we'll run into each other again. I figure there must be a reason he showed himself to me. My neighbor, Mr. Mot, says that maybe the E.B. and I are kindred spirits.*

Anyways, Easter's coming, the Medieval Faire is coming, maybe E.B. is coming. Methinks 'twill be a most splendid April!

CHAPTER IV

The Code of Chivalry

Bee found a Knights' Code of Chivalry on the Internet, printed it out, and brought it to the fort after school today.

"We need one of these," she said, tapping the piece of paper.

"What is it?" asked Jack.

"It's like the rules we promise to follow as knights," said Bee. "For instance, one of them is 'to protect the weak and defenseless.'"

"¡Órale!" said Jack. "That's a good one. What else?"

"'To speak the truth at all times,'" said Bee.

"I'm down with that," I said. "Except for white lies. Sometimes you need white lies."

Bee yanked the pencil out from behind her ear and wrote "white lies" on the piece of paper.

"Ooh, here's a tough one," she said. "'To despise pecuniary reward.'"

"What does that mean?" asked Jack.

"I think it means that we won't take money as a reward," Bee said.

"I like that," was Jack's knee-jerk* reaction. "Let's keep it."

"Wait a second!" I said. "If we do something really nice and considerate, and someone wants to slip us a few bucks as a thank you, are you saying we have to turn it down?!"

"Yyyes," nodded Bee.

It took a while, but eventually we came up with our own list of rules. Bee wrote them down:

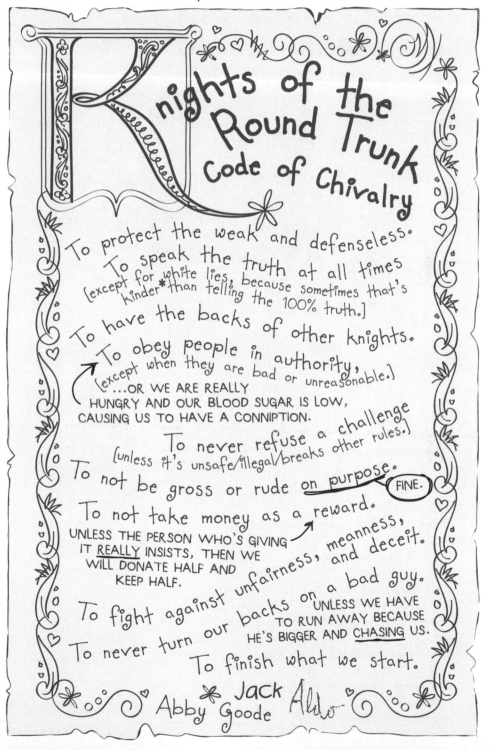

Knights of the Round Trunk Code of Chivalry

To protect the weak and defenseless.

To speak the truth at all times (except for white lies, because sometimes that's kinder*than telling the 100% truth.)

To have the backs of other knights.

To obey people in authority, (except when they are bad or unreasonable.) ...OR WE ARE REALLY HUNGRY AND OUR BLOOD SUGAR IS LOW, CAUSING US TO HAVE A CONNIPTION.

To never refuse a challenge (unless it's unsafe/illegal/breaks other rules.)

To not be gross or rude on purpose. FINE.

To not take money as a reward. UNLESS THE PERSON WHO'S GIVING IT REALLY INSISTS, THEN WE WILL DONATE HALF AND KEEP HALF.

To fight against unfairness, meanness, and deceit.

To never turn our backs on a bad guy. UNLESS WE HAVE TO RUN AWAY BECAUSE HE'S BIGGER AND CHASING US.

To finish what we start.

Abby Goode * Jack Aldo

"OK," said Bee after she'd nailed the Code to our fort tree. "We've got suits of armor and a Code of Chivalry, But I've been thinking... I don't see how we can be knights if we haven't been knighted."

I HEREBY DUB THEE... SIR DUSTJACKET, PROTECTOR OF THE HARDCOVERED.

"Oh, right!" said Jack. "Somebody has to turn us from regular kids into knights. Somebody important. Like the queen. Or a librarian."

"Hmm," I said. "Good point. We can work on that tomorrow. But right now, my trusty stomach says it's dinnertime o'clock..."

We crawled out from under the fort tree and saw that Timothy and Karl were hanging out on the playground again. They must have just finished baseball practice, because they were wearing their jerseys and hats.

"Let's go say hi to them," said Bee.

"Nah," Jack and I said at the same time.

"But we just agreed to never turn our backs on a bad guy!" said Bee. "Besides, maybe Karl's not a knave after all. We can't be unfair, right?"

Reluctantly, Jack and I followed Bee to the playground. Timothy and Karl were swinging on the swings, and as we got closer, Karl called, "You're not gonna steal our jackets this time, are ya?" Their sweatshirts lay in a heap on the ground near the slide.

I'M SO NICE AND ADORABLE, I SHOULD BE ON THE DISNEY CHANNEL.

"No, sillies!" Bee said. "That was just for April Fools' Day."

"I like your costumes," said Karl as he stood up, took off his hat, and smoothed his hair. This time his voice sounded friendly, like water bubbling over happy rocks in a stream.

3

"They're for the Medieval Faire at school," said Jack.

"It's a pretty sweet party they have every year just for 5th graders at Dana Elementary," explained Timothy.

"Oh. Cool," said Karl. "We didn't have anything like that at my old school."

"Hey, Aldo!" Timothy said, hucking his baseball hat in my direction. He was taking it off so he could do hanging-upside-down tricks on the swing. "Put this by my sweatshirt."

Although that is not the proper way to address a king-knight, I carried Timothy's cap over to the sweatshirt heap. As I put down the hat, I noticed something shiny sticking out of one of the sweatshirt pockets. I leaned closer to get a better look.

IT WAS A FANCY SILVER WATCH!

I glanced over at Jack and Bee, who by now were giving Timothy and Karl underdog pushes on the swings. Everyone was laughing and having fun, but for some reason I had a flustery feeling in my stomach that was making my fun-o-meter droop. *Probably just hunger,* I thought.

"Gotta go!" I called and turned to walk home. "Time for dinner, Timothy!"

Time. The watch wasn't Timothy's—I knew that. Probably it was Karl's. A kid with fancy shoes could have a fancy watch too. As I walked up the street to my house, I kept thinking about Karl and how new people amble into your life all the time whether you like it or not. How are you supposed to know if they're good guys or bad guys?

45

I was so lost in my brain questions that I almost missed it. As I shuffled past the clump of bushes between my house and our neighbor's, my eyes spotted a wiggle off to the side, where a wiggle shouldn't be. I turned my head just in time to see a furry white derrière with a fuzzy tail disappear into the gloom under the bushes.

I quick looked around to see if anyone else had noticed. No one. So I dropped to my hands and knees and looked for a bunny. Maybe THE bunny. But the only thing under the bushes was (a) dirt, (b) air, and (c) an empty Big K soda can. *Gah!*

I grabbed the can for recycling because I'm chivalrous like that, checked behind the bushes, then went home for dinner, during which Timothy talked and talked about baseball this and Karl that.

I promise you, I'm not even one fry short of a Happy Meal. I know it was probably just a regular neighborhood bunny I saw today—even though they're usually light brown, not white like this one was. But just in case, since it's E.B. season, I'm keeping my eyes peeled.

CHAPTER V

Killjoy*

You're probably wondering why this knock-knock joke* is not funny. That's because it's not a joke. It's what really happened when we went to Mr. Mot's house after school today! He's my retired English teacher neighbor who loves fancy words. We figured he'd know all the right things to say for a knighting ceremony.

So we banged the knocker* on his door. He opened it. We told him what we wanted. Then he said, "I am sorry, my honorable young friends, but I cannot knight you."

"Why not?" asked Jack.

"We're already wearing the outfits," I pointed out.

"Because ordinary citizens are only made knights after they have done something of great service."

"Ohhh," said Bee. "That makes sense. No problem. We'll just go do something great!"

"Sigh...," I said, slumping my shoulders forward and hanging my head as much as my cardboard armor would let me. "Sounds like a lot of work."

"I bid you enter," said Mr. Mot, opening the door wide. "Perhaps I may be of service to you."

He put a bowl of kettle corn* in the middle of his kitchen table, and we all sat down to brainstorm quest ideas.

"I know!" said Bee. "My mom and I volunteer at the cat shelter. We could all go together and help clean out the litter boxes!"

"Cats are for the weak," I said. "Plus, kitty-litter duty is uber unknightish."

"My *abuelo* lives at the old folks' home," said Jack. "We could go play cards or something with him and his roommates."

"Abuelo's cool," I said.

"A fine idea, indeed!" said Mr. Mot. "I shall offer another. The much-anticipated Jackalope Junction Easter-Egg Hunt takes place this coming Sunday. Alas, it has come to my attention that the open space and playground, where the festive, candy-filled eggs will be tucked away, has the appearance of neglect. BUT!" and here he raised his voice and also his left arm off the table, pointing a finger to the ceiling, "if a company of would-be knights were to spend a mere hour or 2 on Saturday gathering debris and tidying up, the egg hunt would be the thoroughly delightful experience it <u>should</u> be for both the kiddies* and their adult companions."

Blerg. In his long, windy way, Mr. Mot was saying we should pick up trash.

"I'm good with that," said Jack. "I <u>loved</u> that Easter-egg hunt when I was little. It shouldn't be junky."

"It's perfect!" said Bee.

"K,*" I shrugged. "Let's do it."

Bee and Jack both looked at me askance. *Why aren't you disagreeing about a chore that involves doing physical work OUTSIDE?* their faces asked.

"What?" I said. "Our Code of Chivalry decrees we'll never refuse a challenge. I'm a knight of my word."

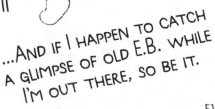

...AND IF I HAPPEN TO CATCH A GLIMPSE OF OLD E.B. WHILE I'M OUT THERE, SO BE IT.

BACON BOY

in KEEP ON KEEPIN' ON

THE "KEEP"* OF A CASTLE WAS THE PART THAT WAS THE KING'S HOUSE. THIS IS BACON BOY'S KEEP (CUT-AWAY VIEW).

THE ROYAL SUN DECK

BEDROOM/ MEDIA ROOM AND LIBRARY

ART STUDIO

KITCHEN AND DINING ROOM

SUPERHERO TRAINING GYM

CHAPTER VI

Trash Talk

One thing I figured out today is that outdoor trash is like annoying big brother habits—the more you pay attention to them, the more you notice.

Even though the sky was dribbling rain, we met Mr. Mot in the field after school. He carried a big plastic trash bag and held it agape while Jack and Bee and I went around picking up weird gobs of garbage and tossing them in.

If you'd asked me before today,
I would've sworn that our
neighborhood was clean. But
this afternoon, when we really
looked, we found gross old
plastic straws and torn-up tennis
balls. We collected bottle caps, popsicle
sticks, and raggedy-yellow sheets of
newspaper. Bee climbed a tree to grab
a shredded plastic bag that was stuck
there. In the ditch we picked up a
muddy, ruined towel
and faded swim
goggles that must've
been forgotten by
a careless
youngster
last
summer.

HEH-HEH...
I FOUND THIS
KRISPY KREME
BOX IN OUR
FORT! CAN YOU
BELIEVE THAT?
KIDS THESE
DAYS!

Near the swings, we spotted some sandy ABC gum and a few cigarette butts.

But the worst part was the dog poop. Can you believe that people take their dogs on Number 2 walks then just leave the dooky wherever it drops?! Good thing Jack was feeling noble.

The whole time we trash hunted, I was secretly hunting for E.B. too, but I saw neither hide nor hare of him.

Finally, after we'd stuffed 2 bags with trash and the Jackalope Junction open space was Easter-egg-ready, Mr. Mot declared that we had performed an honorable deed and were worthy of knighthood. So right there in the field, Jack and Bee and I knelt* down and Mr. Mot turned us into official knights.

HERE YOU DO REAFFIRM YOUR OATH OF FEALTY AND SERVICE TO YOUR FAMILY, FRIENDS, AND NEIGHBORS. YOU DO HEREBY SWEAR BY MOUTH AND HAND TO BE GOOD AND WORTHY KNIGHTS, TO BE EVER COURTEOUS AND REVERENT, TO SEEK EXCELLENCE IN ALL YOUR ENDEAVORS, TO BE COURAGEOUS AND FAITHFUL, TO BE ALWAYS LOYAL AND TRUE, TO TEMPER JUSTICE WITH MERCY, TO BE TEMPERATE AND HUMBLE, TO SHELTER THE WEAK, TO HELP THE NEEDY, TO CHAMPION THE RIGHT, AND UPHOLD THE GOOD. SO SWEAR YOU?

¡SÍ!

OF COURSE!

HUMBLE TOO? SHEESH.

I DUB THEE SIR LOPEZ, DAME GOODE AND SIR ZELNICK. ARISE AND GO FORTH IN CHIVALRY.

I was starting to arise and go watch TV when I noticed I'd almost kneeled in a handful of tiny pooplets. Not doggy doo this time—bunny nuggets!

I was wondering *Does the Easter Bunny go to the bathroom?* when my thought movie got paused by a ferocious loose dog. He came running onto the field, tearing this way and that, barking at us like crazy. He was dirty-white with long, dreadlocky hair. None of us knew him.

BEE'S LITTLE SISTER, VIVI, HAS A PET RABBIT. THAT'S WHY I CAN DIAGNOSE THEIR DOO-DOO.

"He must be lost. C'mere, boy!" tried Bee. She clapped her hands and whistled, trying to get him to calm down and come to her. But he kept his distance, and he also kept bark-bark-barking.

LOOK! A MOP WITH A MOUTH!

"I cannot see a collar or tag," said Mr. Mot over the cacophony. "Perhaps we should call the Humane Society."

Suddenly Psycho Dog went quiet and froze like a statue. His ears perked forward, and his keen* eyes stared at a group of bushes on a grassy knoll* past the slide. We all turned to look, too, to see what was so interesting.

In the shadowy darkness near the bottom of one of the bushes, I thought I saw something stir, like maybe a piece of paper fluttering. Only there wasn't any paper under those bushes. I'd cleared out all the trash there myself...

WHAT IS THAT???

Oh no, I thought. E.B.!

The dog and I bolted for the bushes at the same instant. He beat me. By the time I got there, he'd sniffed every square inch around and under them 3 times. The good news is that he didn't have a white bunny—or anything—clamped in his killer jaws. The bad news is that he was now coming for <u>me</u>.

Psycho Dog barked and snarled and darted toward me. I swung my sword back and forth at large-dog level and closed my eyes. (Have you ever noticed that sometimes even <u>looking</u> is too scary?)

Then *whew*, Sir Jack came charging full-tilt.

With a confident, "Begone, cur!", he brought down the flat of his sword on the dog's keister, and the conquered mutt finally took off.

"Whoa, I thought I was a goner," I said. "Thanks."

"No big deal," said Jack. "Just having your back and sheltering the weak. You know."

"Hey, I'm not weak!" I argued. "Did you notice how I was the first one to race over here?"

"Yeah, what was that all about?" asked Bee. "You actually <u>ran.</u> Sort of."

Luckily, Mr. Mot halted this conversation by inviting us to his house for celebratory kefir.* While we drank, there was gabbing about what our next quest should be, but I wasn't paying much attention. I was busy imagining what I will say to E.B. when I finally do meet him face-to-face.

CHAPTER VII
GUITAR HEROES

At my house, Friday night usually means two things: (1) Mr. Mot and my dad play electric guitar in the basement. (They're both into oldies rock 'n roll.); and (2) The rest of us— including my mom and Goosy and sometimes Timothy and our friends—pile onto the family room couch and watch a movie. It's how we all unwind after a hard week of school and whatever it is grown-ups do during the daytime.

Jack and Bee came over for tonight's movie because it was *The Holy Grail*, which is about medieval times and knights and King Arthur and how banging coconuts together sounds like running horse feet. It's so hilarious, even Timothy and Karl quit playing *MLB: The Show* on the Playstation upstairs and joined us. (That's a baseball video game. Yes, Timothy is such a superjock that he even plays sports when he's not playing sports.)

By the end of the movie, though, I was getting so tired that I couldn't even eat any more popcorn. I stood and stretched. It was time for Jack and Bee to go home and me to go to bed. My mom turned off the TV. On the floor, Timothy and Karl had started a quiet but intense push-up contest.

Mr. Mot and my dad emerged from the basement door and headed over to us.

BEFORE YOU KIDS CALL IT A NIGHT, THERE'S SOMETHING WE WANT TO TALK TO YOU ABOUT.

WE'VE LEARNED OF A NEED IN OUR COMMUNITY, AND WE THOUGHT THAT A COMPANY OF KNIGHTS SUCH AS YOURSELVES COULD BE OF GREAT SERVICE.

"Groan," I groaned. "I'm exhausted."

"Mr. Mot and I know a fantastic keyboardist,*" continued Dad, ignoring my exhaustion. "His name is Lucas, and he plays in a band called Kerfuffle.* Anyway, he's a professional musician, not garage banders like me and Mr. Mot. But he was in a car accident this week and broke his arm."

"Ow," I said. "That hurts." I should know because I broke my arm a few months ago.

"Ow indeed," said Mr. Mot. "Yet the problem is not so much the pain as it is the loss of income. You see, Lucas's wife just had a baby. She is not working right now so that she can stay home to care for the infant. And Lucas cannot play the keyboard for at least a month, until his arm heals. So what the young family needs is a little financial assistance."

I pulled my pockets inside out to show my lack of financial money. Karl slid his wallet from his back pocket and tried to hand my dad a $20 bill.

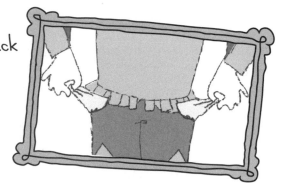

"No," said Dad, waving off Karl's cash. "That's very generous of you, Karl, but we aren't asking you kids for money. Mr. Mot and I were thinking we could hold a fundraiser, and all of you could help."

"What a marvelous idea!" exclaimed Goosy, jumping to her feet and clapping. "What should we do?"

So, despite my obvious fatigue, Mom got out a big piece of paper, taped it to the wall, and all of us spent a few minutes brainstorming a list of ideas (guess which person thought of which idea):

FUNDRAISER IDEAS

- ☐ Car wash
- ☐ Make and sell friendship bracelets
- ☐ Art raffle
- ☐ Read-a-thon
- ☐ Bake sale
- ☐ Kissing booth
- ☐ Circus
- ☐ Spring yard clean-up service
- ☐ Dunk tank
- ☐ Donation jars at Bee's family's restaurant
- ☐ Kaleidoscope* making
- ☐ Eating contest
- ☐ Spelling bee
- ☐ Baseball lessons
- ☐ Family photos

After we finished the list, we debated which ideas would work the best, i.e., raise the most funds, then we voted. Luckily for my taste buds, the bake sale won. And we're going to have the bake sale on Sunday, during the Jackalope Junction Easter-Egg Hunt, which is only two days from now!

That means that tomorrow, Saturday, the Zelnick family kitchen will be churning out cookies and cakes and baked goods galore. My dad, who's probably the world's greatest cook, is in charge. The rest of us will assist.

Just think—a bakery in my own house! It's a dream come true, really. Goodnight. If you need me, I'll be nestled in my bed with visions of sugary goodness dancing in my head.

CHAPTER VIII

THE KING WAS IN HIS COUNTING HOUSE, COUNTING ALL HIS YUMMY.

First thing this morning, Dad shook me awake from a dream about medieval doughnuts. I opened my eyes to see him standing next to my bed with a piece of paper in his hand. He held it out to show me the long list of supplies we needed to go get for the day's baking project.

So off we went to Costco. In case you've never been, Costco is one of those hockey-stadium-sized stores where you can buy flour in sacks as big as me and pretzels by the million. Dad and I filled our ginormous cart with flour, sugar, butter, eggs, oatmeal, cocoa powder, coconut, nuts, vanilla, cream, Easter-color M&Ms, some other stuff, and a few extra baking pans.

When it was time to pay, Dad opened his wallet and realized he didn't have as much cash as he thought he did. Uh-oh. But then he remembered the ATM machine outside, so he ran to get more money. Soon we were all checked out and back at our house, and Dad was ready to get his baker on.

First he rounded up his helpers: me, Jack, Bee, Timothy, Karl, Goosy, Mr. Mot, and Mom. He handed each of us an apron, then he split us into teams of one kid and one grown-up. But there was an uneven number of people, so I ended up on a 3-person team, with Goosy and, *blerg*, Karl, who said he wanted to keep wearing his black sweatshirt with a red dragon on it instead of the apron.

Dad assigned my team kiffels.* They're a traditional Zelnick family holiday cookie. Kiffels are Hercules-level hard to make, but Dad said the bake-sale shoppers would go gaga for them because they're special. (Have you ever noticed that "special" pretty much always means more work? Why is that?)

The kiffel team set up on one end of the kitchen island and the lemon-bar team (Mom and Bee) on the other end. Dad and Jack used the kitchen counter space to get got going on Easter M&M cookies, and Mr. Mot and Timothy took over the eating table to make chocolate cupcakes. Double batches all around.

BAKING
DAY GAME
PLAN:

TEAM
CUPCAKE:
Mr. Mot
Timothy

TEAM
LEMON
BARS:
Claire
Bee

TEAM
KIFFEL:
Goosy
Aldo
Karl

SUPPLY
HOME
BASE

TEAM M&M COOKIES:
Leo & Jack

The kitchen clanked with measuring cups and grred with mixers. Goosy showed me and Karl how to make the kiffel dough, then Karl rolled it out into a big, flat square because his teenager muscles are supposedly bigger than my 11-year-old ones.

As he leaned forward, Karl's sweatshirt pocket gaped open, and tunneled deep inside it was a white paper cylinder filled with brown crumb-y stuff. A cigarette! My mom told me you have to be 27 and live in your own house to buy cigarettes! How did Karl get cigarettes?! He's only 16! I shot a "Grown-Up Alert" glance at Goosy, but she didn't notice.

"This is cool!" said Karl as Goosy showed him how to cut the rolled-out dough into little squares. "I'm glad I got off work today so I could help with this instead."

"You have a job?" asked Goosy.

"Yep," said Karl. "Part-time at Kinetic fitness center. Cleaning up locker rooms and stuff like that."

"And you play baseball and go to school? What a hardworking young man you are!" Goosy beamed. "Aldo, isn't Karl a prince?"

I had two choices: (1) tattle about the cigarette, which would be telling the knightly truth in answer to Goosy's question...but which would also cause a kerfuffle right there and then in the middle of our baking project, or (2) tell a white lie so our work wouldn't be interrupted. I decided that getting ready for the bake sale and making money for Lucas's family was more important than straight-up honesty. I picked option number 2.

"Yeah, quite a prince," I said in a voice as flat as the kiffel dough.

Karl frowned at me, but Goosy kept kiffeling. "Does your family make a special holiday cookie?" she asked Karl as she opened a can of the apricot jelly we use to fill the kiffels.

Karl's expression changed again, from maddish frown to saddish frown. "Not really," he shrugged.

"Well, Aldo loves kiffels," Goosy went on. "And Easter's a special holiday for him because he once met the real live Easter Bunny." She winked at me. "That's why we Zelnicks make kiffels at Easter."

I closed my eyes and face-palmed. As Goosy launched into the story of The Time Aldo Saw The Easter Bunny, I defected to Team Cupcake, but I could still hear Karl's guffaws from across the room.

Yet I kept on helping. After all, I had to Finish What I Started. By the middle of the afternoon, we were covering paper platefuls of cookies, cupcakes, and lemon bars with plastic wrap and stacking them on the table.

Baked goods baked. Bad guy identified (but not conquered). I'd say that's plenty in Aldo Zelnick's good deeds column for one day. Now it's time for an activity that involves sitting or lying down, preferably with pillows.

HOW TO MAKE KIFFELS

THOSE UBER-DELICIOUS COOKIES FROM ALDO ZELNICK'S "K" SKETCHBOOK

HERE'S WHAT YOU'RE GONNA NEED:

DIFFICULTY LEVEL: ◆◆ BUT WORTH IT

2 ½ TSP YEAST

2 ½ CUPS BUTTER SOFT

1 CUP MILK

4 EGG YOLKS

1 TBSP LEMON JUICE

5 TO 6 CUPS FLOUR

1 TSP SALT

1 CUP SUGAR FOR ROLLING

3 CANS APRICOT FILLING

1. WARM THE MILK AND STIR THE YEAST INTO IT. SET ASIDE.

2. IN A BIG BOWL, USE A MIXER TO WHIP THE BUTTER.

3. MIX THE EGG YOLKS AND LEMON JUICE INTO THE BUTTER.

4. STIR THE SALT INTO THE FLOUR.

5. MIX TWO CUPS OF THE FLOUR MIXTURE INTO THE BUTTER MIXTURE. ADD SOME MILK AND MORE FLOUR MIX. CONTINUE ALTERNATING FLOUR AND MILK UNTIL ALL THE MILK AND 5 CUPS OF THE FLOUR ARE USED UP.

6. IF THE DOUGH SEEMS TOO WET, KNEAD* IN SOME OR ALL OF THE LAST CUP OF FLOUR.

7. SPLIT THE DOUGH IN HALF, WRAP IN PLASTIC, PUT IN FRIDGE FOR 1 HOUR.

8. ROLL HALF OF THE DOUGH ONTO A FLOURED SURFACE TILL EVEN AND FLAT, ABOUT 1/8-INCH THICK.
LIKE THIS:

9. CUT ROLLED-OUT DOUGH INTO 1-INCH SQUARES.

10. DOT EACH SQUARE WITH A BLOB OF APRICOT FILLING. FOLD BLOBBED DOUGH SQUARES.
LIKE A TINY COOKIE TACO:

B
A

11. ROLL UNBAKED COOKIE IN SUGAR.

12. PLACE ON UNGREASED COOKIE SHEET. BAKE AT 400° FOR 6 TO 8 MINUTES.
WATCH BECAUSE THEY BROWN QUICKLY!

13. REMOVE FROM OVEN AND PLACE ON COOLING RACKS.
EAT IMMEDIATELY.

CHAPTER IX
When life gives you lemon bars

A whole herd of families took part in the
Jackalope Junction Easter-Egg Hunt this morning.
The sun was shining. The yellow flowers that look
like this and the red flowers that look like this were
blooming. The grass was green, and
thanks to me and Jack and Bee, trash-
and poop-free. The little kids ran
around gripping empty Easter baskets
and squealing with delight every time
they found another plastic egg.

It was a scene straight out of my childhood.

Jack and Bee and I looked on as we personned the bake-sale table.

"Remind me again...," I said to Jack. "How come we can't hunt eggs anymore?"

"Because it's for kids 10 and younger."

"But you're still 10!" I realized.

"My birthday's next month," said Jack. "I'm basically 11."

"I'll be 12 pretty soon," said Bee.

"Geez. I didn't realize the double digits were going to be so much work and so little play. Is this what grown-ups mean by 'the other side of the hill'?" I wondered out loud as Bee sold a plate of lemon bars to ancient Mrs. Kestrel.

"Look how much money we're bringing in!" exclaimed Bee. She opened the lid of the cash box so we could see inside. She was right. It was starting to overflow with good old American greenbacks.

About then Karl and a man ambled over. My mom and dad walked up to the man and started chatting. Karl came to the bake-sale table.

"See any Easter bunnies this morning, Aldo?" Karl said. He softly play-punched my shoulder. "Just kiddin'* ya. I love the Easter Bunny too."

I rolled my eyes to show my coolness, but I also took a furtive look around the field for white fuzziness. Nothing.

"Is that your dad?" Bee asked Karl.

"Yeah," he said "Where's Timothy?"

"Probably still in bed sleeping," I said. "You should go wake—"

But I didn't get to finish because I was interrupted by ferocious barking. That big white dog was back, bounding amuck around the egg-hunt area and scaring all the little kids! Parents hustled to scoop up their toddlers. Bee's little sister, Vivi, tripped and spilled her basket. She started to cry.

"You guys watch the food and money," said Jack. "I got this."

"I'll help!" cried Bee, chasing after him.

"OK, I'll stay and protect the important stuff!" I said to no one, because by then Karl had grabbed a plate of lemon bars and sprinted in the dog's direction too.

"That'll be 2 dollars!" I called after Karl, but he ignored me. As he ran, he tore the plastic wrap off the plate and threw it on the immaculate ground. That was at least strike 3.

By now more kids were crying, and more parents were trying to catch the hairy monster. Mr. Mot held his megaphone to his mouth and kept repeating, "Everyone, please calm down! Quiet soothes the savage beast!" Goosy had grabbed a leash and fishing net from our garage and joined the chase. My dad was doing one of those earsplitting, 2-fingered whistles. My mom was frozen in place with both hands clamped over her agape mouth.

The egg hunt had gone kerflooey.* It was a kerfuffle, all right.

But when he finally got near the boisterous mutt, Karl halted. He knelt on the ground and held out a palmful of mooshed lemon bar. And whaddya know, the dog stopped barking, loped over to Karl, and literally began to eat out of his hand.

Whew.

Next, one of the egg-hunt families circled around Karl and the dog, who, it turned out, belongs to them! See, they've been having trouble with their backyard gate staying closed, and Keystone—that's the dog's name—has gotten loose a few times lately. He's not so well-mannered when he's an escapee, but once you have him on a leash, he's super amiable. A little later, when his family came over to the bake-sale table, I petted his strange, ropey hair. He licked my face, which just might have contained a kiffel crumb or 2.

After the egg hunt was over and the last treats plate sold, Jack and Bee and I walked to my house and dumped the money we'd collected onto the living-room floor. We put the coins in a pile, the 1s in a pile, the 5s in a pile, etcetera, then we counted the piles and added them up. 497 dollars! We high-5ed and ran to tell the grown-ups. My mom took a picture of us holding the loot.

"I hereby challenge thee to add 3 dollars to make it an even $500," Jack said to me.

"Of my own?"

"Aye."

"Don't forget: you have to accept a challenge," reminded Bee. "It's in the Code."

"OK, fine." I stomped upstairs and dug 12 quarters out of my coin jar.

WE PUT THE $500 IN A PLASTIC BAG AND GAVE IT TO MY DAD FOR SAFEKEEPING.

Tomorrow Dad's going to take me to the bank to trade in the random coins and wrinkly money for 5 crisp $100 bills. Then we're going to figure out a time that we can all go together to Lucas's house to give him and his family the raised funds. I can't wait to see their jubilant faces!

YOU GUYS BROUGHT HOME THE BACON, ALL RIGHT. AND NOW YOU'RE GONNA SHARE IT. NICE!

CHAPTER X

TAKE THAT TO THE BANK

After school today, Dad and I drove to the bank, parked, and went in. I'd never been inside a bank before. Usually when my parents have banking errands, we do the drive-through. Until today, I thought banks were basically like KFCs except with money instead of fried chicken.

The bank insides were kinda like a church—all seriousness and high ceilings and grown-ups in dressy clothes. We approached the fancy wooden counter and handed the loot bag over to the lady. She had on an official-looking name tag, so I figured it was kosher.* She counted the money then slid us 5 crisp, handsome $100 bills.

BY THE WAY, GUESS WHICH PRESIDENT IS ON A $100 BILL:

GEORGE WASHINGTON

THOMAS JEFFERSON

THEODORE ROOSEVELT

BARACK OBAMA

ALDO ZELNICK

GIVE UP? TURN TO PAGE 90 FOR THE ANSWER!

With our new bills safely tucked into an envelope safely tucked into my dad's shirt pocket, we were turning to leave when a man's voice called, "Well hello, Zelnicks!"

It was Karl's dad. He was wearing a business suit and tie, shiny black shoes, and one of those official-looking name tags. He's a banker! No wonder Karl is rich! He shook my dad's hand, then he held out

his hand to shake mine. (*Sigh.* In the double digits, you're also expected to have grown-up manners.) Then I slumped down into a nearby lobby chair because I knew the start of a Long, Boring Adult Conversation when I heard one.

"Blah, blah, blah, blah...blah, blah, blah." I noticed a water machine and went to get me a cup. I came back to more "Blah, blah, blah." I pulled up my socks and checked my pockets for lint. "Blah, blah, blah." I picked up a magazine from a table and pretended to read an article about king penguins.*

Then I overheard Karl's name and tuned in to the dadversation.

"Karl sure came to the rescue when that dog went crazy!" my dad was saying.

"Yeah, he's a good kid," said Mr. Knight. "But he's been having kind of a hard time lately. What with the move here... And his mom's not in the picture, you know..."

"Sorry to hear that," said my dad. "That's tough. But that also reminds me... Claire and I were hoping you and Karl could join us for Easter dinner on Sunday. I'm a capable cook, if I do say so myself."

"Sounds fantastic!" said Mr. Knight. "The only thing I know how to cook up is reservations."

"We'll see you at 2 in the afternoon, then," said Dad. "Dress casual. Maybe we can get in a game of kickball* after we eat."

On the ride home, my eyeballs were gawking out the window, but my brain was thinking about Karl not having a mom in the picture. What does that mean, exactly? Jack's parents are divorced, but they live close to each other, and he ping-pongs back and forth between them all the time. If a mom's "not in the picture," does that mean she kicked the bucket*? Or she's living in Kathmandu*? Or she's a Russian spy? Or she just hates having her picture taken? What if _my_ mom wasn't in _my_ picture...

We were almost home when a flash of white near the fort tree caught my attention. "Stop!" I yelled.

My dad slammed on the brakes, and my seatbelt gave me a little strangle. "What's wrong?!" he panicked.

"I have to go check something!" I managed to choke out. "I'll meetcha at home!" I jumped from the car and ran. (What's with all my running lately?)

I circled the fort. Nothing. I crawled under the branches into the inner sanctum. Nothing. I was slithering out when I found it: a jumbo clump of white fur caught on a poky branch. I picked it off and inspected it. Was it E.B.'s? I sniffed it. It didn't smell like jelly beans or chocolate...

Hmm. I stuffed the fur into my pocket and headed home. Maybe later I can find a way to figure out which animal it belongs to. But right now, it's chowtime. BRB.

ANSWER FROM PAGE 86:

IT'S ALL ABOUT THE BENJIS

NONE OF THE ABOVE! ACTUALLY, NO PRESIDENT IS ON A $100 BILL. THAT'S BECAUSE BENJAMIN FRANKLIN IS! EVEN THOUGH HE WAS AN EXTRAORDINARY DUDE, HE WAS NEVER THE PRESIDENT. AND NOW YOU KNOW WHY HERE IN THE GOOD OL' U.S. OF A., $100 BILLS ARE SOMETIMES CALLED "BENJAMINS."

Over chicken kebabs* at dinner we talked about when to give Lucas the money. Mom said she'd already discussed it with Mr. Mot, Goosy, and Karl's dad, and the first day everyone can get together is this Friday. So we agreed that on Friday, we'll bring Lucas's family a golden egg like in that Willy Wonka movie, only this one will be a plastic egg filled with the 5 $100 bills.

Mom gave me a plastic gold egg. I opened it, fastidiously rolled up the Benjamins, placed them inside it, then closed the egg.

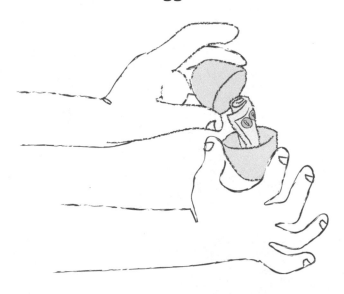

Dad told me to take the egg upstairs and put it in his sock drawer. If you ever need to borrow/steal something valuable from the Zelnick residence, now you know where to find it.

p.s. This Runescape Knight's Sword game I've been playing online lately is a good way to get your medieval chivalry fix without having to mess with any actual effort or heroics.

CHAPTER XI

Good Fencers make Good Neighbors

After school this afternoon Mr. Mot gave
the Knights of the Round Trunk a fencing lesson.
In case you didn't realize, fencing does not mean
building a fence. Because that would be extremely
boring. And fatiguing. It means...swordfighting!

"I studied the ancient art of fencing when I was in the Navy," said Mr. Mot. "We were fortunate to have occasional shore leave in Italy, and whenever I wasn't delighting in the *Biblioteca Angelica* library in Rome, I was learning how to fence from the best swordsmen in all the world."

Using our cardboard swords, we learned how how to lunge and parry, which basically means to attack and to defend yourself from an attack.

Since I'm ambidextrous, I can swing my sword equally well with either arm. Mr. Mot says that's rare and could help me win a duel. Too bad the bottom half of my body is so klutzy.*

MY NAME IS ALDO ZELNICK! YOU STOLE MY KLONDIKE BAR! PREPARE TO DIE! WHOA-OA-WHOOPS!

Speaking of imaginary Klondike ice cream bars, after a while my stomach realized that it must be getting close to dinner. "Welp!" I called. "That's enough activity for today! Time to make like a king and start wal<u>king</u> home. Get it?"

"Thou must depart so soon?" asked Mr. Mot. "Why, it seems it's only..." He paused mid-parry and glanced at his left wrist. "Alas, I keep forgetting that my watch is missing. Dost thou know the hour?"

"It's 5:30," said Bee. "I should go too."

"Fare thee well, my good men and lady!" said Mr. Mot. "I shall see you anon! And if thou should'st come across my good silver watch, which I seem to have misplaced, I pray thee, return it to me! I offer a $10 reward!"

Oh boy. Oh man. A "good silver watch." Missing. The truth was dawning on me like the sun in the morning sky, only faster. Instead of going home, I motioned for Jack and Bee to follow me to our fort.

OMYGOSH! YOU KNOW WHAT JUST DAWNED ON ME? UNDERSTANDING!

"I think I know where Mr. Mot's watch is," I whispered when we were safe inside. "I saw it in Karl's sweatshirt pocket that day you guys were pushing Timothy and Karl on the swings."

"You did?" gasped Bee.

"Yep. And there's more. Remember how Karl pulled a 20-dollar bill out of his own wallet that night we watched *The Holy Grail?* He wanted to give it to my dad for Lucas's family, but then my dad wouldn't take it?"

"Yeah, I remember...," said Jack.

"Well, the next day my dad and I were at Costco getting ingredients for the bake sale," I continued, "and when we were checking out, money was missing from my dad's wallet!"

"You think Karl stole money from your dad?" asked Bee.

"Then offered to give it back to him?" asked Jack. "That's brazen."

"Maybe," I said.

"But Karl has a job, right?" said Jack. "He earns money."

"True," I said. "And his dad is a banker. So they're rich..."

"How do you know Karl doesn't have his own silver watch?" asked Bee. "Just because he has a nice watch and 20 dollars doesn't mean he's a thief." She pulled the Code of Chivalry off the tree trunk. "This says we'll fight against unfairness, meanness, and deceit. Maybe you're being unfair and kinda mean to Karl right now, Aldo."

"Maybe," I repeated dubiously. "But he almost attacked you when you April Foolsed his shoes... And I have 2 more things to tell you. (1) I found out that Karl's mom is out of the picture. (2) When we were baking, I saw a cigarette in Karl's pocket."

"Ew!" said Bee.

"It coulda been a piece of string cheese," shrugged Jack, who (a) loves string cheese, and (b) never likes to think the worst of anyone.

"It was a cigarette," I repeated knowingly.* "I'm sure because afterward, I looked up a picture of one on the Internet. I just can't figure out how he got it. You have to be a grown-up to buy them, don't you?"

"Yes," said Jack. His dad's a fireman, so he's in the know* about everything fire-and-smoke-related. "You have to be 18. But someone older could have given him one."

"Hey!" cried Bee. "When we picked up trash with Mr. Mot, we found cigarette butts near the playground slide, remember? That's right where we've seen Karl and Timothy hanging out sometimes!"

"But Karl isn't a bad guy," defended Jack. "He helped us with the bake sale. And he rescued all those little kids from Keystone. And if his mom is out of the picture...that's sad."

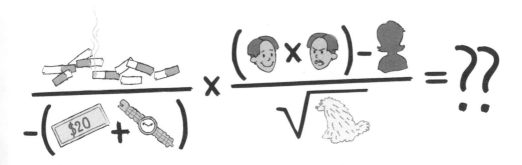

I'M PRETTY MUCH AN EINSTEIN AT MATH, BUT THE KARL EQUATION IS JUST TOO COMPLICATED FOR ME TO SOLVE.

Now it was time for silence to dawn. We sat quietly for a few minutes, trying in our minds to make all the pieces add up. They didn't really.

"I think," Bee said finally, "that Aldo should bring this up with Timothy first. Before we tell the grown-ups what we think might be happening, we should try to understand what's really going on. After all, we promised to 'speak the truth at all times.' We need to find out what the truth <u>is</u>."

Groan. "You want me to ask Timothy if his new best friend is a kleptomaniac* and a smoker too?" I said. "That'll go well."

"It's the right thing to do, Aldo," said Jack. "Or, better yet, you could go straight to Karl and ask him."

"Timothy it is!" I agreed. "I'll let you know what he says." And even though it was dinnertime, I headed home reluctantly.

Timothy and I ended up at the mall after school today because Mom made us shop for Easter clothes. Which is bad enough, but she also makes us try things on. Why is it that moms think the world will end if you don't try before you buy? To figure out if clothes will fit, you just hold them up in front of you. Duh.

In the men's dressing room, Timothy was in one stall, and I was in the next. We each had a pile of pants and shirts Mom "helped" us pick out. She told us to try them on 1 at a time then walk out to the mom area to show her. *Blerg.*

I grabbed a pair of pants from my stack and got started. I couldn't see Timothy, but I could hear him tapping away on his iPhone.

"You're supposed to be putting on clothes, not texting," I complained as I tried to zip and button.

"Shutup," he replied all fast, like it was 1 word instead of 2.

"You're not allowed to say that," I grumbled. I pulled on the second pair of khakis.* These were even tighter. My mom seems to forget I'm 11 now. I listened for trying-on noises from Timothy's direction. Nothing. "You'd better get going!" I said.

"Shutup," he repeated.

Between Timothy and the stupid pants, I was getting pretty annoyed. Annoyedness makes you braver, I've noticed. So I blurted out, "Karl stole Mr. Mot's watch, didn't he?"

"What??" said Timothy. Now his voice sounded like it was coming from the sky, like God's. I looked up and saw him glaring down at me.

"Mr. Mot's good silver watch is missing," I said. "And that day when you and Karl were on the swingset, I saw a fancy silver watch in his sweatshirt pocket."

"So?" said Timothy. "Karl probably has one too."

"And also," I went on, still burning annoyedness jet fuel, "Dad noticed money missing from his wallet, and Karl had a $20 bill." OK, that one was feeble. Even I could tell that.

"Karl's not a stealer. You're dumb," Timothy concluded as he dropped back down into his own stall.

"Plus!" I cried. I'd saved the knockout* punch for last. "I saw a cigarette in Karl's pocket."

Timothy Superman-leaped into my stall in a single bound. He was discombobulated for some reason.

"When we were baking."

He leaned against the wall, crossed his arms, and eyeballed me. His apprehensive expression changed to superjock game face. "Nah, there was no cigarette," he said at last. "You're making that up. Or you were hallucinating."

"No, I wasn't!" I said. *Was I?*

"Well, it's your word against Karl's," he shrugged. "You've got no proof."

I looked down. My bewildered big toe poked out from a hole in my left sock. Timothy was right. I don't really have proof that Karl is a bad guy. Maybe that's cuz he isn't.

"Tell ya what, kiddo,*" soothed Timothy. He cuffed me gently on the shoulder. "I'm gonna go show Mom my outfit and tell her you need bigger pants. I'll bring you the pants, and you can model for her. Then I'll talk her into getting us kung pao chicken* take-out for dinner. How's that sound?"

Good. That's how it sounded. Actually, better than good. Kissable.*

In a flash Timothy returned with pants I could close. He went back into his stall to try on one final pastel shirt.

"Hey, Timothy?" I said. My question floated up and over the stall wall and down to my big brother. "How come Karl's mom isn't in his picture?"

"I don't know really," said Timothy. "Well, he did mention once that his mom moved to Kansas when he was little. Like, for a job or something. Maybe she wasn't a baby person."

"Weird," I said and got ready to go model the shirt and pants I detested the least. "But he's not a baby anymore. It'd be safe for her to come back now."

On the way out of the mall, Mom carried the clothes bags, Timothy carried the Chinese take-out sack, and I carried my unsureness about what I was gonna report back to Jack and Bee about Karl. We walked right past a guy in a giant Easter Bunny suit. He was there to give kids hugs and high-5s and for parents to take pictures. It wasn't E.B., of course, but Mom still caught my eye with a look and a sideways head nod that meant, "There's the Easter Bunny, Aldo! Do you want to go say hello?"

I glowered and kept on walking. Moms. You can't live with 'em; you can't live without 'em. Well, you can, but...

IT'S SO HOT IN THIS SUIT I'M ABOUT TO KEEL OVER*...

CHAPTER XIII

THE GOBLET OF AWESOMENESS

Today at school we made our goblets for the Medieval Faire. What's a goblet, you ask? It's a fancy drinking cup—one fit for a king. Or a knight. Or a wizard.

Our teacher, Mr. Krug, gave us each a clear plastic cup with a fancy stand part. Like this:

Then we brushed the outside with gold paint and glued on glitter and bogus jewels. We left the insides plain so they can be drunk from.

While we slaved away, Mr. Krug read aloud to us from *The Sword in the Stone* book. He took a break from reading at one point to have a conversation with my mom, who had stopped by to talk with him about the Medieval Faire (she's coordinating the parent volunteers). I used the moment to fill in Bee and Jack about what Timothy said about Karl.

"Timothy said Karl's not a klepto," I whispered. "And he finagled us Chinese food. Oh, and he said I was hallucinating the cigarette."

"Were you?" asked Jack.

"Nope. But maybe it's <u>his</u> business if he wants to kill his own respiratory system."

"So...he's a good guy then," said Jack slowly.

"Or at least <u>mostly</u> a good guy," said Bee.

"I guess so." I shrugged and glued one final fake ruby onto my goblet.

After school I walked home with Jack, like usual. When we got to his mom-house, I told him I wanted to see the new rocks in his collection—a kind (and necessary) white lie.

"You do?!" He was flabbergasted with joy.

"Sure," I said. "Like, do you have some kryptonite* or something?"

We started up the stairs to his room. "Dude," he gushed, "my Pebble Pal in Sweden sent me a shard of kammererite.* It's super rare, and—"

I stopped him. "Wait a second. What's a Pebble Pal?"

A ROCK? IN THE MAIL? KINDA DUMB.

"Oh, it's like a pen pal for rocks. We mail each other small specimens from our locations. I've got Pebble Pals in New Zealand, Maine, Kazakhstan*...a bunch of places. Check out this coal from Kentucky! It's their state mineral and..."

I kindheartedly* oohed and ahhed for a minute then suggested an after-school snack would be most welcome. "Would you mind making us peanut-butter sandwiches so I can stay here and keep studying your collection?" I asked.

Jack was so ecstatic to think he might be encouraging a new rock hound that he didn't even hesitate. He grinned and took off kitchen-ward. I, meanwhile, hustled over to his desk, fished the white-fur clump from my pocket, and placed it on his microscope platform. I flicked on the light and peered through the lens.

Here's what I saw:

Magnified 400 times, the hair looked kinda like little beads strung together in a necklace. But was it E.B. fur? I couldn't tell. I don't know what I was expecting. It's not like it was gonna be labeled "Easter Bunny fuzz" in miniature letters. Then I heard Jack bounding back up the stairs, so I grabbed the clump and was just re-pocketing it when he burst into the room.

"You're looking at rocks under the microscope?!" he cried with delight. He handed me my sandwich.

"Just trying to figure out which one to examine first," I white-lied again. "Heh-heh."

"I know!" he agreed. "It's so hard to choose!"

Jack began lining up stones for me to inspect, chattering all the while about mineral this and crystal that. *Blerg.* I had to gawk at quite a few before I was able to excuse myself and head home.

Just two-and-a-half more days till Easter. Maybe E.B. will reveal himself to me then. Or maybe E.B. magic only works on single-digit kids. *Sigh.*

CHAPTER XIV

BAD FRIDAY

eople say that bad things come in 3s. After today, I'm pretty sure they're right.

The first bad thing happened during school lunch. We were having chili, and I thought it would be funny to stick a kidney bean* in each nose hole and recite one of the quotes from *The Sword in the Stone* that Mr. Krug made us memorize:

"PERHAPS HE DOES NOT WANT TO BE FRIENDS WITH YOU UNTIL HE KNOWS WHAT YOU ARE LIKE. WITH OWLS, IT IS NEVER EASY-COME, EASY-GO."

OK, it <u>was</u> funny. Jack and the friends laughed their 5th-grade heads off. That's cuz everything's funnier with beans in your nose...until the beans get stuck and you have to go see Nurse Dolores. When she tweezered them out—and some nose hairs came too—I definitely did <u>not</u> laugh.

Then after school, Jack and Bee wanted to try jousting, but since they didn't have horses and lances handy, they had to use bikes and foam pool noodles. I judged. Jack was right when he predicted he would be a good jouster.

That's when Karl and Timothy came along. Karl said he wanted to fight the winner, so after Bee lost the first match, Karl climbed on Bee's bike, and he and Jack took a run at each other. Guess what happens when a competitive teenager and a skinny, not-competitive 10-year-old ride their bikes straight at each other and the 10-year-old turns at the last second, only instead of turning <u>away</u> from the teenager, he accidentally turns <u>into</u> the oncoming teenager's path.

Bad thing number 2, that's what happens. Jack and Karl ended up in a knot* of bikes and legs and arms. Karl yelled at Jack for running into him. Jack cried. Bee scolded Karl for being a bully. Timothy gave me his disgusted "Why do you and your friends have to be such babies?" look. Yes, it was a mini-kerfuffle—but nothing compared to the jumbo kerfuffle to come.

The first 2 bad things were separated from the 3rd bad thing by an intermission of goodness. My dad had cooked up big batches of kielbasa* and homemade mac-and-cheese because Karl and his dad plus Goosy, Mr. Mot, Jack, and Bee were eating with us. After dinner we were all going to Lucas's house to give his family the money we'd raised for them!

The combination of the mac-and-cheese and the good-deed-doing-to-come put all of us kids in a happy mood again. I saw Jack, whose proudness had been hurt more than his body, show Karl the piece of kammererite in his pocket. Timothy brought me a key-lime* soda. Bee couldn't stop grinning in anticipation. Then it was time to go visit Lucas.

"Sport, run upstairs and grab the egg," said Dad.

So I hustled to Dad's sock drawer and yanked it open. I plunged my hand into the sock nest and felt around in the right back corner, where we usually keep anything special. All I felt was socks. I walked my fingers around the entire bottom of the drawer. Nothing. I used both hands to scoop the socks out onto the floor until the drawer was empty. No egg. It was <u>gone</u>.

"THE GOLDEN EGG ISN'T HERE!" I started shouting as I turned back and headed down the steps. "THE GOLDEN EGG IS MISSING!" Everyone gathered at the foot of the stairs and looked up at me.

"It's gone?" asked Mom.

"Yes!" I wailed.

"Timothy, have you seen it?" asked Dad.

"No," said Timothy.

"Does anyone have any idea where it could be?" asked Goosy.

For a while, no one said anything. The silence was so thick you could have cut it with a cardboard sword. Inside of me, I could feel the pressure building up like a volcano. Actually, it had been building up for a couple of weeks now. It was time for me to blow like Krakatoa.*

"Karl took it!" I accused loudly. "He's a thief and a knave! Karl, give it back!" I was glaring and yelling directly at him by this point. "That money is for a poor family, not a rich kid!" I was out of control. I was going berserk. I was kingsize* crazy and I knew it.

"Aldo, the Code says no conniptions, remember?" Bee loud whispered, but instead I ran right at Karl and began lunging with my sword.

BEWARE, KARL THE KNAVE, FOR YOU HAVE AWOKEN THE FEARSOME WRATH OF SIR ALDO ZELNICK, KNIGHT OF THE ROUND TRUNK, A.K.A. KING VALENTINE!

"Take that!" I thrust. "And that!" I whacked. My ambidextrous fencing skills were really coming in handy. Karl finally got hold of my sword and tore it from my hands. His eyes were as big as kaiser rolls,* and they looked kinda watery...

Dad picked me up by the back waist of my jeans. He put me in the coat closet. He closed the door. "Aldo, you need a time-out," he said through the door. "Just for a minute. Until you calm down. Breathe..."

From my coat prison I could hear Karl saying, "I didn't take it! I wouldn't do something like that!"

I busted out of the closet. "Yes, you would!" I hollered. "You stole Mr. Mot's watch! You took money from my dad's wallet! And you <u>smoke cigarettes!</u>"

The room hushed again. In my now-silent fury, I noticed that Bee had her arms crossed over her chestplate, and her face was as red as those silly beets she plants in her garden. Jack had started crying for the 2nd time today. Mr. Mot wore a teacherly expression of concern. Goosy's eyes and mouth stood open in big Os. And Timothy... well, the weird thing is that Timothy looked... apprehensive.

Mr. Knight turned to Karl. "You stole a watch?" he asked. "And money?"

"No!" said Karl. His face scrunched up into a fierce grimace. "I didn't steal anything!"

That set me off again. I couldn't help it! "You're a liar liar liar liar liar liar liar!" I yelled in my fight against unfairness, meanness, and deceit. This time Dad carried me upstairs to my room. "Liar liar liar liar liar liar!" I kept yelling the whole way.

Dad set me on my bed and told me to stay here. Which is where I am now, sketchbooking my guts out.

This is not over, Karl Knight. Ohmygosh, your name is Karl Knight. *Gah!* That is so ironic I want to start conniptioning again! But I will remain calm. Even though I am obeying people in authority right now by not leaving this dungeon, I am not turning my back on you, Karl. Somehow I am going to get that $500 back and make sure Lucas's family receives it. My true inner knightliness has been kindled.* I <u>will</u> finish what I started.

IT'S LIKE ANYTHING IN LIFE, ALDO. THERE ARE GOOD KNIGHTS, AND THERE ARE BAD KNIGHTS.

OK, Mom and Dad finally came into my room to tell me that everyone went home.

"And we understand why you were upset," said Mom, "but you behaved very, very badly."

_I_ behaved badly?

"But—," I started to say.

"Button it," said Dad in his mad voice, which he almost never uses. "We don't know who did what, but Karl and his dad are going to talk things over tonight, and the rest of us are going to get some sleep. Tomorrow, when everyone's cooled off, we'll figure out what really happened. Now goodnight."

Mom kissed me on the top of my head, and that was that.

I tried texting Jack and Bee, but my phone died and the charger's downstairs. At least I have Max. And my betta fish, Bogus. And E.B.?

CHAPTER XV

FROM ONE KNAVE TO ANOTHER

When I woke up this morning, the first thing I remembered was the missing $500. I'd fallen asleep mad, but overnight, my madness had turned to sadness. I hate when that happens. Cuz sadness hurts more.

I lay there for a while, floundering in my grief. Then I finally dragged myself out of bed and shuffled down to the kitchen. In keeping* with my mood, the kitchen stunk like it does underneath my covers after bean-burrito dinner. That's cuz Dad was hardboiling eggs.

Jack and Bee stood waiting for me. "We're ready to go on a quest to get the money back from Karl," said Jack. Bee nodded.

But then the doorbell rang. It was Karl and his dad! My mom led them into the kitchen.

My heart kerflopped,* but before another kerfuffle could break out, Mr. Knight laid his hands on Karl's shoulders, and Karl's face got ready to talk. This was it. The moment of Truth.

"I'm sorry," Karl said softly. "I'm sorry I've been mean to Aldo and his friends a couple times. But I didn't steal a watch. And I never took any money. I saved up to buy my Kapers shoes myself." He held out his wrist. "This watch is mine. My mom sent it to me for my 16th birthday. It's a knockoff,* but I like it."

"It's a nice watch," sniffed Jack, wiping his cheek. "I bet it's good at telling time."

"Thank you for coming to talk to us this morning," said my mom, and she gave Karl a quick side-hug.

Even I had to admit that Karl seemed to be telling the Truth. But then what had happened to the $500?

"Karl, there's one more thing you have to tell the Zelnicks," urged Mr. Knight. "Go on, son."

Karl threw Timothy a look of silent misery. Timothy closed his eyes and face-palmed.

"I'm sorry I brought cigarettes to your house," murmured Karl, who was now looking down to study his Kapers. "And...I'm sorry I gave some to Timothy."

What?! My annoying but otherwise flawless brother had demolished his superjock lungs with cigarettes?!

I'M KNEE-DEEP* IN TROUBLE...

"OK, well, we'll talk to Timothy about that later," said my dad, squeezing Timothy's shoulder. There was a lot of shoulder squeezing going on. "Thank you for coming to explain things, Karl. And Aldo, now it's your turn to apologize to Karl."

I sighed. Then I looked at Karl and said, "I'm sorry for thinking you were a knave. Even though you are, a little bit, kinda. And most of all I'm sorry that the golden egg is still missing." We could all apologize till the cows came home, but without the $500, it was all just kvetching.*

Still, all of us found a way forward by coloring real Easter eggs (and previewing tomorrow's candy).

While we dipped and dripped, we talked about what could have happened to the $500. Theories ranged from actual burglars to Max ate it to alien abduction. We also discussed what we could do to raise <u>another</u> $500.

Just then my mom's scream bounced down the hallway and into the kitchen. It wasn't her "There's a snake in the bathroom!" scream. (That one is bloodcurdling.) This was her "Oh my gosh! What a great surprise!" scream.

She came sprinting into the kitchen with a fistful of wadded-up paper.

In her hands were the 5 Benjamins! No longer fastidiously rolled up. No longer crisp. But still $500.

It turned out that the plastic golden egg halves were also in the dryer. So were a pair of my pants. I guess I'd been distracted by the Runescape Knight's Sword game on my computer that day. I must have pocketed the egg, which never even made it to Dad's sock drawer. Instead, it's been in the dirty-laundry chute all week!

"Oops," I said to everyone. "Sorry about that." I felt heavy with humiliation and kielbasa digestion. But at the same time I felt a tug of lightness because Lucas's family will get the $500 after all. I looked around the room and saw lots of different expressions on people's faces.

Timothy's face did not brim with brotherly love, but Karl's look was soft with knave-to-knave kinship.* "That's OK," he said to me. "The money's been found. That's what matters."

"Get out the iron, Aldo," said Mom. "You're going to press these bills until they're as nice as you can make them."

Jack and Bee helped me iron the Benjamins and put them back into the golden egg. The egg delivery trip to Lucas's house has been postponed until tomorrow after Easter church but before Easter dinner.

Now if only E.B. shows up tomorrow morning, all will be right with my kingdom.

CHAPTER XVI

A Tisket A Tasket

I woke up in the weak, gray light of early morning and glanced around my room. No E.B. I crept downstairs to the family room, where two chock-full Easter baskets sat waiting—one for me, one for Timothy. No E.B., though. I ran to the window to see if I could catch him hopping down the bunny trail. Nothing.

Now I'm lying on the couch and eating chocolate eggs from Timothy's basket as medicine for my disappointment. I really thought this was gonna be the year of The Second Time Aldo Saw The Easter Bunny.

Mom woke me from my couch nap and said it was time for church. So I got dressed, and we all went to Easter services, which are packed with people and singing and flowers and girls in frilly dresses. I sat between my mom and Goosy. Timothy slid way down to the opposite end of the pew. Since yesterday, he's been acting like I'm the knave.

After church Bee and Jack came over. We put on our knight costumes. Karl and his dad and Mr. Mot joined us, and our mostly merry company marched across the egg-hunt field to the apartment building where Lucas and his family live. We mounted the stairs and rang their doorbell.

Once everyone was introduced, Jack and Bee and I handed Lucas their special Easter basket filled with kiffels and other goodies...and the golden egg. Mr. Mot told them about the bake-sale fundraiser and how, on account of Lucas's broken arm, we wanted to help.

Then Lucas's wife, Kendra, popped open the golden egg. She gasped and put her hand over her mouth. After that came a tornado of Thank you!s and ¡Gracias!es and You're welcome!s and hugs, handshakes, and kisses. Even their little baby, Camila, slobbered on my cheek.

Now I think I finally understand what a real knight feels like.

Then, on the walk back home, 2 more good things happened.

Jack noticed something shiny hanging on a bush branch and bent to pick it up. It was Mr. Mot's watch! Mr. Mot said it must have fallen off that day we picked up trash. He thanked Jack, got out his wallet, and handed him the $10 reward.

But the 3rd good thing was the most unexpected of all. We were passing by our fort tree when I saw another flicker of white fuzz under the branches. *E.B.! Finally! You didn't forget me after all!* I crawled inside the fort. Curled up there in the cardboard box we use as a fort table was a mama cat and 5 teeny-tiny kittens!

The kittens were all different colors, but the mama cat was big and pure white and fuzzy. And she had a short, fluffy tail!

"So <u>you're</u> the white fuzzball I've been glimpsing all month," I whispered. I reached out to pet the mama cat. She rubbed the top of her head against my palm.

By then Jack and Bee were alongside me. "She's a bobtail!" cooed Bee. "And she doesn't have a collar or tag!"

"She's so friendly!" said Jack. "She must be lost!"

We carried the boxful of cat-and-kittens with kid gloves* out to show the teenagers and grown-ups. Then we took the box to Bee's house. Bee's mom said she would drive the mama and babies to the cat shelter to be examined by the veterinarian. We can visit them there tomorrow.

So today we rescued Lucas's family, Mr. Mot's watch, and 6 cats. All in a knight's work. I guess good things can happen in 3s too.

p.s. In case you're wondering, we had ham for Easter dinner. Followed by a kickball game in which Timothy kept booting the ball straight at me whenever he got the chance.

p.p.s. I've decided a mama cat and kittens in the hand is worth 2 E.B.s in the bush any day.

CHAPTER XVII

The Cat Castle

Today after school Bee's mom took us to the cat shelter, which is in an old, castley-looking building made of stone on the edge of town. It turned out that the fuzzy white mama cat <u>was</u> lost. She belongs to a family who was looking for her. Her name is Kismet!

Kismet will live at the shelter for a couple of months, though, until her babies are old enough to go home with other families. I held the yellow kitten today. She's so itty-bitty she fits in the palm of my hand, but when I softly stroked her with 1 finger, she purred for me! I'm gonna ask my parents and Max if we can adopt her.

In other news, Jack donated <u>all</u> of his $10 reward to the cat shelter. And besides being grounded, Timothy's punishment for trying cigarettes is that he has to teach a class about how smoking hurts your body. Mom and Dad said I have to be his student. Bee and Jack are invited too. So we have <u>that</u> to look forward to.

CHAPTER XVIII

Medieval Faire

Cue the trumpets! At long last the day of the Medieval Faire cameth, and it was most splendid and joyful!

The Dana Elementary gym became our castle game room. We 5th graders spent the morning there trying medieval activities at different stations. There was juggling, shield making, Merlin's magic relay, balloon swordfighting, and even medieval karaoke* in a booth manned by Mr. Mot. (Remind me to tell him that Gregorian chanting is not the best party music. He might want to put the kibosh* on that for next year's Faire.)

Outdoors on the school soccer field were more boisterous activities, like pool-noodle jousting (this time on foot instead of bikes), a bouncy castle, and Capture the Flag, which of course I avoided like the plague. Mom was off in one quiet corner showing kids Frightful, the peregrine falcon who had a broken wing that couldn't be totally fixed and lives at the raptor center these days.

tournament field

A JUGGLING JESTER... AM I IN THE RIGHT BOOK?

At lunchtime all us 5th graders paraded up and down the hallways of the entire school so the little kids could cheer and clap for us. We made our way to our classroom, which had magically been transformed into a castle keep complete with giant chandeliers hanging over long banquet tables. There we feasted on meats, crusty bread, hunks of cheese, roasted potato fingers, and raw veggies.

After lunch we went outside again for that special dance Bee foretold. We stood in two rows facing each other, and while old-timey music played over the loudspeaker, we clapped, stepped, touched hands, and spun, all in a certain order. That is not as easy or enjoyable as it sounds. Then we took turns whacking a dragon piñata. When at last Marvin cracked it open, chocolate coins wrapped in golden foil rained down upon us.

"The Medieval Faire was everything I dreamed of and more," sighed Bee on our walk home.

"It was great," said Jack. "But being real knights for a few weeks... that was greater."

"All I know," I yawned, "is that <u>this</u> king-knight is in need of a catnap."

"Speaking of cats, did your parents say you could have the yellow kitten?" asked Bee.

"Yep. When she's old enough. And I thought of the perfect name for her: Kerfuffle."

"But you said cats are for the weak," remembered Jack.

"No I didn't," I white-lied. "Also, Karl is adopting the mostly black kitten with white paws."

"That seems right," said Bee.

"Yep," I repeated in agreement. "That seems like just the right end to this kinda foolish, kinda heroic tale."

"K" GALLERY

Mr. Mot used to be an English teacher. He's a word nerd, and he likes to help me use awesome words in my sketchbooks. I mark the best words with one of these: * (it's called an asterisk). When you see an * you'll know you can look here, in the Gallery, to see what the word means. If you don't know how to say some of the words, just ask Mr. Mot. Or someone you know who's like Mr. Mot. Or go to aldozelnick.com, and we'll say them for you.

K (pg. 51): yes. Short for "OK." (Because "OK" is too long?)

K.O.-ing (pg. 21): knockout-ing

ka-ching (pg. 79): cash-register sound that means "lots of money"

kahunas, big (pg. 16): the chiefs, bosses, or kings of a group

kaiser rolls (pg. 120): yummy, large sandwich buns

kale (pg. 18): a leafy green veggie that's supposed to be good for you

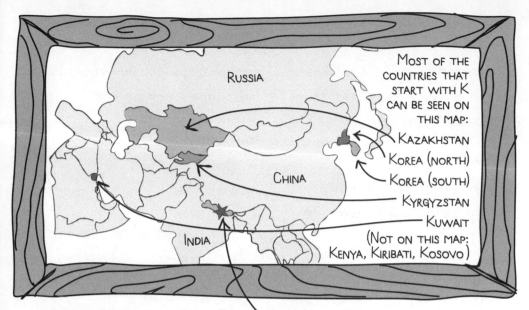

MOST OF THE COUNTRIES THAT START WITH K CAN BE SEEN ON THIS MAP:
KAZAKHSTAN
KOREA (NORTH)
KOREA (SOUTH)
KYRGYZSTAN
KUWAIT
(NOT ON THIS MAP: KENYA, KIRIBATI, KOSOVO)

kaleidoscope (pg. 66): like a telescope but instead of seeing stars, you see colorful shapes

kammererite (pg. 110): a purple crystal rock

kangaroo (pg. 11): I'm pretty sure you know what a kangaroo is.

kaput (pg. 7): done; finished

karaoke (pg. 7): singing with a microphone like you're a star

karma (pg. 122): the luck you deserve

Kathmandu (pg. 89): the capital of Nepal

Kazakhstan (pg. 111): the biggest "stan" country; between Russia and China

kebabs (pg. 91): meat on a stick! One of the smaller meat family you can eat while walking around.

keel over (pg. 107): pass out

keen (pg. 59): sharp and paying attention

keep (pg. 52): the king's house part of a castle. It "keeps" the king. Get it?

keeping, in (pg. 126): in a way that fits the circumstances

kefir (pg. 61): drinkable yogurt. Too healthy to be a real celebration beverage.

keister (pg. 9): butt; derrière. Rhymes with Easter.

kettle corn (pg. 49): popcorn with salt and sugar on it!

kerflooey (pg. 81): to fall completely apart

kerflopped (pg. 126): a funner way to say "flopped"

kerfuffle (pg. 64): a commotion; a brouhaha; a big fuss

Kerplunk (pg. 29): a game with pointy sticks and marbles in a plastic tube

ketchup (pg. 25): a delicious tomatoey condiment

key-lime (pg. 117): a tiny lime that tastes like a lime

keyboardist (pg. 64): someone who plays the keyboard, which is an electronic piano

SOME FOODS ARE WORTH GETTING KEYED UP ABOUT.

keyed up (pg. 28): super-excited

khakis (pg. 102): tan dress pants. Khaki is the color.

kibble (pg. 25): dry pet food

kibosh (pg. 139): stop doing something; put an end to

kickball (pg. 89): a game like baseball except you kick a big, bouncy playground ball

kickboxing (pg. 33): a fighting sport that involves kicking and hitting

kicked the bucket (pg. 89): bit the dust; bought the farm; died

kicks (pg. 20): shoes

kickstart (pg. 7): get something going

kid gloves (pg. 136): handle something really carefully

kiddies (pg. 51): little kids

kiddin' (pg. 79): jokin'

kiddo (pg. 105): what an older person calls a younger person when he's trying to be nice

kidney bean (pg. 114): a red bean that's shaped like your kidneys

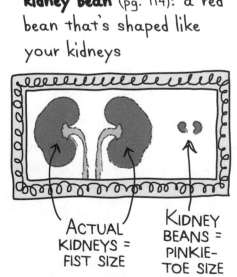

ACTUAL KIDNEYS = FIST SIZE

KIDNEY BEANS = PINKIE-TOE SIZE

kielbasa (pg. 117): a delectable Polish sausage

kiffels (pg. 70): only the best cookie ever!

killjoy (pg. 47): a person who wrecks other people's fun

kinder (pg. 41): nicer

kindergarten (pg. 15): the official start of many long years of required school

kindheartedly (pg. 111): doing with niceness

kindled (pg. 123): got going; lit an enthusiasm fire for

kindred spirits (pg. 37): beings that have a special connection or bond

king penguins (pg. 87): the second-biggest kind of penguin. (Emperor penguins are biggest.)

kingpin (pg. 101): the guy in charge

kingsize (pg. 119): extra-large

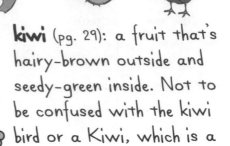

kink (pg. 53): cramp

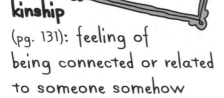

AOOO-GAH!

kinship (pg. 131): feeling of being connected or related to someone somehow

kiosk (pg. 10): a stand that sells things

kissable (pg. 106): when you like something so much you feel like kissing it

kitschy (pg. 32): some people think it looks nice, but really it's kind of ugly or tacky

kitty-corner (pg. 23): across from sideways; cattywampus

kiwi (pg. 29): a fruit that's hairy-brown outside and seedy-green inside. Not to be confused with the kiwi bird or a Kiwi, which is a person from New Zealand.

klaxon (pg. 122): an uber-loud horn that blares when there's an emergency

kleptomaniac (pg. 100): a person who gets a kick out of stealing stuff. "Klepto" for short.

klutzy (pg. 95): not graceful; uncoordinated

knack (pg. 25): naturally good at something. By the way, words that start with "kn" in English are always pronounced like the K isn't there. Weird.

knave (pg. 8): a person you can't trust; a bad guy

knavery (pg. 32): bad things a bad guy does

knead (pg. 76): smoosh over and over with your hands

knee-deep (pg. 128): deeply; way a lot

knee-jerk (pg. 39): automatic; without thinking

kneel (pg. 27): sit on your knees

knelt (pg. 57): sat on your knees; same as "kneeled"

knick-knack (pg. 32): a fragile decoration that just sits there gathering dust

knish (pg. 27): a hand-pie with meat and potato filling; kind of like an empanada, only Jewish. Also, this word is an exception to the silent K rule. It's pronounced "kuh-NISH."

knock-knock joke (pg. 48):

KNOCK KNOCK.

WHO'S THERE?

A BROKEN PENCIL.

A BROKEN PENCIL WHO?

NEVER MIND. IT'S POINTLESS.

knocker, door (pg. 48): one of those heavy metal door-banger things

knockoff (pg. 127): something that's made to look exactly like an expensive item, but it's actually cheap and a fake

knockout (pg. 104): the final blow

knoll (pg. 59): a little hill usually covered in grass

knot (pg. 116):

PARDON ME, BUT ARE YOU A STRING?

WHY, NO, I'M A FRAYED KNOT.

know, in the (pg. 99): educated about

knowingly (pg. 99): with understanding and wiseness

knuckleball (pg. 34): some kind of baseball pitch for knuckle-heads

knucklehead (pg. 8): someone who makes bad choices. Like a knave, except a knave is intentionally bad and a knucklehead is more accidentally bad

kohlrabi (pg. 160): kooky cabbage

Komondor (pg. 9): a breed of dog with ropey white hair covering its eyes

kooky (pg. 22): weird; bizarre

kosher (pg. 86): legitimate; copacetic

kowtower (pg. 31): Sounds like → Means someone who acts meek and mild and servant-like.

Krakatoa (pg. 119): one of the most explosive volcanoes ever

kryptonite (pg. 110): a rock from the pretend planet Krypton in the Superman stories. Kryptonite is Superman's only weakness.

kumquat (pg. 7): an orange the size of an olive

kung pao chicken (pg. 105): delicious chicken in a spicy-sweet sauce with peanuts and those hot red chili peppers that you shouldn't eat but if you accidentally do, they K.O. you

kvetching (pg. 128): complaining. Like "knish," this is another one of those K words where you pronounce the K separate from the rest of the word.

liege (pg. 31): an early "L Gallery" entry that is a term of respect for a king; rhymes with prestige

I'LL SEE YOU KNUCKLE-HEADS IN *LOG JAM*, MY NEXT SKETCHBOOK!

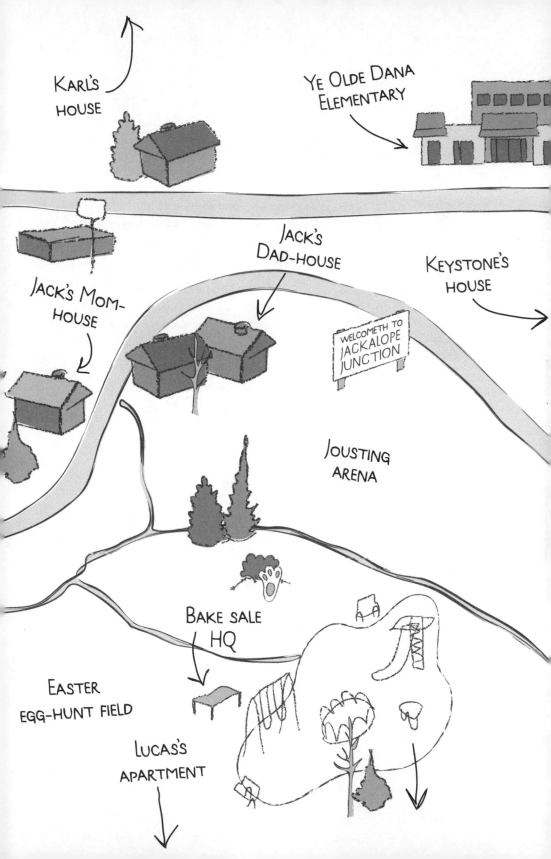

ABOUT THE award-winning ALDO ZELNICK COMIC NOVEL SERIES

The Aldo Zelnick comic novels are an alphabetical series for middle-grade readers aged 7-13. Rabid and reluctant readers alike enjoy the intelligent humor and drawings as well as the action-packed stories. They've been called vitamin-fortified *Wimpy Kids*.

NOW AVAILABLE!

160 pages | Hardcover
ISBN: 978-1-934649-04-6
$12.95

Part comic romps, part mysteries, and part sesquipedalian-fests (ask Mr. Mot), they're beloved by parents, teachers, and librarians as much as kids.

Artsy-Fartsy introduces ten-year-old Aldo, the star and narrator of the entire series, who lives with his family in Colorado. He's not athletic like his older brother, he's not a rock hound like his best friend, but he does like bacon. And when his artist grandmother, Goosy, gives him a sketchbook to "record all his artsy-fartsy ideas" during summer vacation, it turns out Aldo is a pretty good cartoonist.

In addition to an engaging cartoon story, each book in the series includes an illustrated glossary of fun and challenging words used throughout the book, such as *absurd, abominable*, and *audacious* in *Artsy-Fartsy* and *brazen, behemoth*, and *boisterous* in *Bogus*.

BAILIWICK PRESS

www.bailiwickpress.com | www.aldozelnick.com

ALSO IN THE ALDO ZELNICK COMIC NOVEL SERIES

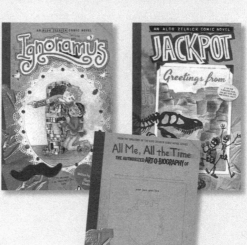

ACKNOWLEDGMENTS

*"Defend the weak, protect both young and old,
never desert your friends. Give justice to all, be fearless in
battle and always ready to defend the right."*

— Brian Jacques, The Law of Badger Lords

Trouble is, what is "right" can be a murky matter, indeed. It's all well and good to march out into the world with noble intentions, but where you expect to find good versus evil, black or white, you are much more likely to discover infinite gradations of gray. What say you then?

Still, the hearts of children and grown-ups alike never cease kerflopping for tales of knights and knaves, kings and kingdoms. As lovers of story and literature, we are just as besotted by everything medieval as the rest of you, and so we set out to add a modern-day Arthurian tale to the Aldo Zelnick canon.

Verily, a company of unequivocally good men and ladies attended us on *Kerfuffle*. We thank kindred-spirit interns Daniel George and Matt Ryder, keen copyeditor Jessie McCoy, *Lord of the Rings* devotée Renée, kickbutt designer Launie, and the Slow Sanders—including and in remembrance of Jerry, who in his last months provided comments on this very manuscript and who always got a kick out of the Aldo series yet thought Aldo himself rather knavish.

King-size kudos, too, to our our kith and kin and to Aldo's kindhearted Angels, all of whom help carry our knapsacks on this long and kooky alphabetical quest.

ALDO'S KINDHEARTED ANGELS

Halo There! If you're an Aldo Zelnick fan, e-mail info@bailiwickpress.com and ask for details about becoming an Aldo's Angel. Angels receive special opportunities such as pre-publication discounts, free shipping, naming rights, and listing in the acknowledgments (especially fun for kids).

Barbara Anderson

Carol & Wes Baker

Butch & Sue Byram

Michael & Pam Dobrowski

Leigh Waller Fitschen

Chris Goold

Roy Griffin

Bennett, Calvin, Beckett & Camden Halvorson

Oliver Harrison (Matthew & Erin)

Terry & Theresa Harrison

Richard & Peggy Hohm

Chris & Diane Hutchinson

Vicki & Bill Krug

Annette & Tom Lynch

Lisa & Kyle Miller

The Motz & Scripps Families (McCale, Alaina, Everett, Caden, Ambria & Noah)

Kristin & Henry Mouton

Jackie O'Hara & Erin Rogers

Betty Oceanak

Jackie Peterson and Emma, Dorie & Elissa

John Schiller & Suzanne Holm

Slow Sand Writers Society

Barb & Steve Spanjer

Dana Spanjer

Vince & Adrianne Tranchitella

THE ALDO ZELNICK FAN CLUB
IS FOR READERS OF ANY AGE WHO
LOVE THE BOOK SERIES AND
WANT THE INSIDE SCOOP ON
ALL THINGS ZELNICKIAN.

GO TO WWW.ALDOZELNICK.COM
AND CLICK ON THIS FLAG-THINGY!

SIGN UP TO RECEIVE:

- sneak preview chapters from the next book.
- an early look at coming book titles, covers, and more.
- opportunities to vote on new character names and other stuff.
- discounts on the books and merchandise.
- a card from Aldo on your birthday (for kids)!

The Aldo Zelnick fan club is free and easy.
If you're under 13, ask your mom or dad to sign you up!

ABOUT THE AUTHOR

Karla Oceanak has been a voracious reader her whole life and a writer and editor for more than twenty years. She has also ghostwritten numerous self-help books. Karla loves doing school visits and speaking to groups about children's literacy. She lives with her husband, Scott, their three boys, and a cat named Puck in a house strewn with Legos, ping-pong balls, Pokémon cards, video games, books, and dirty socks in Fort Collins, Colorado. This is her eleventh novel.

ABOUT THE ILLUSTRATOR

Kendra Spanjer divides her time between being "a writer who illustrates" and "an illustrator who writes." She decided to cultivate her artistic side after discovering that the best part of chemistry class was entertaining her peers (and her professor) with "The Daily Chem Book" comic. Since then, her diverse body of work has appeared in a number of group and solo art shows, book covers, marketing materials, fundraising events, and public places. When she invents spare time for herself to fill, Kendra enjoys skiing, cycling, exploring, discovering new music, watching trains go by, decorating cakes with her sister, making faces in the mirror, and playing with her dog, Puck.